I Love You Rhymes

Cover illustration by JON GOODELL

Illustrations by
LISA BERRETT
KRISTA BRAUCKMANN-TOWNS
JANE CHAMBLESS WRIGHT
DREW-BROOK-CORMACK ASSOCIATES
KATE STURMAN GORMAN
JUDITH DUFOUR LOVE
BEN MAHAN
ANASTASIA MITCHELL
ANITA NELSON
ROSARIO VALDERRAMA

Louis Weber, C.E.O.
Publications International, Ltd.
7373 North Cicero Avenue
Lincolnwood, Illinois 60646

Manufactured in U.S.A.

8 7 6 5 4 3 2 1

ISBN: 0-7853-1647-7

PUBLICATIONS INTERNATIONAL, LTD.

Rainbow Books is a trademark of Publications International, Ltd.

Lavender Blue

Lavender blue and rosemary green,
　　When I am king you shall be queen;
Call up my maids at four o'clock,
　　Some to the wheel and some to the rock,
Some to make hay and some to shear corn,
　　And you and I will sing until morn.

Curly Locks

Curly Locks, Curly Locks,
   Will you be mine?
You will not wash dishes
   Nor yet feed the swine,
But sit on a cushion
   And sew a fine seam,
And feed upon strawberries,
   Sugar, and cream.

Why May I
Not Love Jenny

Jenny shall have a new bonnet,
   And Jenny shall go to the fair,
And Jenny shall have a blue ribbon
   To tie up her bonny brown hair.

And why may I not love Jenny?
   And why may not Jenny love me?
And why may I not love Jenny
   As well as another body?

Boy and Girl

There was a little boy and a little girl
    Lived in an alley;
Says the little boy to the little girl,
    "Shall I, oh, shall I?"
Says the little girl to the little boy,
    "What shall we do?"
Says the little boy to the little girl,
    "I will kiss you."

The Deer

The deer he loves the high wood,
    The hare she loves the hill;
The knight he loves his bright sword,
    The lady—loves her will.

Burnie Bee

Burnie Bee, Burnie Bee,
    Tell me when your wedding will be.
If it be tomorrow day,
    Take your wings and fly away.

He Loves Me

He loves me.
   He don't!
He'll have me.
   He won't!
He would if he could.
   But he can't.
So he don't.

I Shall Be Married

Oh, Mother, I shall be married to
   Mr. Punchinello,
To Mr. Punch,
   To Mr. Joe,
To Mr. Nell,
   To Mr. Lo,
To Mr. Punch, Mr. Joe, Mr. Nell, Mr. Lo,
   To Mr. Punchinello.

I Love Coffee

I love coffee,
 I love tea,
I love the girls,
 and they love me.

Fiddle-De-Dee

Fiddle-de-dee, Fiddle-de-dee,
   The fly shall marry the bumblebee.
They went to church, and married was she;
   The fly had married the bumblebee.

My Love

Have you seen my love
    Coming from the market?
A peck of meal upon her back,
    A baby in her basket;
Have you seen my love
    Coming from the market?

Molly, My Sister

Molly, my sister, and I fell out,
    And what do you think it was all about?
She loved coffee and I loved tea,
    And that was the reason we couldn't agree.